"Great is the power of steady misrepresentation, but the history of science shows that fortunately this power does not long endure."

Charles Darwin

This book is a work of fiction. Any references to historical events, real people, or real places are used fictitiously. Other names, characters, places, and events are products of the author's bizarre and sometimes warped imagination. Any resemblance to actual events or places, or persons, dead or alive, is entirely coincidental.

For theatrical or film rights, contact the author at kylepberry@gmail.com.

The Invitation

A short story by

Kyle P. Berry

In the middle of a brutal winter night, five strangers are drawn to a Chicago bar by a mysterious invitation. Why are they there? What compelled them to go? As the night unfolds, the reason becomes clear. But can these strangers go on living with what they now know?

The 116 Club

In Chicago, January of 2019 brought some of the worst weather the city had seen in decades. Power grid failures, rising utility costs coupled with bitterly cold temperatures caused most Chicagoans to become hermits and stay indoors. *Most Chicagoans*, but not all.

Located on the city's trendy north side, J's Bar was an old-school establishment past its prime. The pub was once a hotspot for Millennials and Generation Xers, but those days were long gone. Just five years prior, it was one of the more popular places to hang out or meet after work for a drink and live music. It was now somewhat out of place in a neighborhood filled with high-end clothing shops, trendy restaurants, and group fitness studios. J's Bar had become an eyesore.

Inside the dingy bar, a few round tables were scattered around, and all but one of them was empty. Chairs were placed upside down on top of all the other tables. A handful of barstools were lined up and pushed in and under the bar's weathered wooden ledge. One of the barstools was occupied by a woman, while two men sat at the only clean table.

Up against the wall opposite the bar, a very well-worn Golden Tee video game sat unplugged while a dartboard precariously hung on the wall a few feet away.

The layer of dust that had built up on most of the surfaces throughout the bar would cause one's allergies to kick into overdrive.

A TV hung high up on the wall, nestled in the corner of the room. The low definition signal the television was managing to receive was showing a nature program. The volume was muted to allow mellow music to be heard in the background.

The bartender wiped down the counter and cleaned the inside of four shot glasses. On one of the coldest nights on record in Chicago, four people were gathered in this depressing bar.

"Six below wind chill! Why do we live here again?" asked one of the men.

"Kids!" another man replied.

"I really hate this weather," the bartender interjected. "But, these shots should warm us up," he added as he poured the liquor into the shot glasses.

"Can't we switch it up this year? I mean, *Jägermeister*? Does anyone even *like this stuff*?" One of the men complained. The others disagreed with this point of view. As if they were going to change things now.

"Ok, ok, I know; it's tradition," admitted the man.

"And it would be bad luck to change our annual toast now. I mean, it's been five lucky years for us, so we can't screw up our mojo because of one little shot of nasty licorice every year," said the lone woman, who appeared to be on her way to or from work.

"That's right, honey!" said the bartender as he leaned over the bar to kiss the woman.

"Ok, raise your glasses, boys," she said.

The bartender walked around the bar and joined the others as they stood and raised their glasses for their traditional toast.

"May this day serve as our annual reminder that loose lips sink ships and that we are only as strong as the bond we share through common secrets. Until next year - The 116 Club!" she toasted.

"The 116 Club!" the others replied in unison.

Mr. Not Relevant

Back in 2014, times were a lot easier. There wasn't a recession in sight, unemployment was relatively low, and the Cubs were a bit less sucky. And Chicagoans, just like most of the country, were reveling in a booming economy.

It was another cold and windy January night in Chicago. Not quite one of the harshest on record, but close. It was miserable - the type of cold where your nose hairs freeze, your ears hurt, and most cars plainly refuse to start. Humans weren't meant to live in these conditions, but Chicagoans were used to it.

Rocco's Pub was a staple for many 30 and 40-somethings on the North Side of the city. Made famous for its dart tournaments, karaoke nights, and post-Cubs game drink-fests, Rocco's was the place to be. Casual and understated, it was a neighborhood favorite.

But this night was an unusual one for this hotspot. It was nearly empty. A sign on the front door indicated that someone had rented out the place for a private party.

Paula, the bartender and owner, had received a rental contract that included the entire bar for the night of January 16, 2014. It was a bit of a mystery to her, however. The person had paid in cash.

A few weeks back, Paula arrived at the bar to get ready for the day when she found an envelope under the door with her name on the front, a contract, and $800 in cash. The renter's name only said 'Gordon R.' No phone number or email or any other way to get in contact with him.

But this was a Tuesday night, and even with how crowded Rocco's typically was, Tuesdays were always the worst days of the week. Maybe Gordon R. knew this, or perhaps he didn't care? Either way, Paula was happy to take the $800 and close the bar for the night. This private event was about double what she'd make on an average Tuesday night in January, and tonight was anything but average. The wind chill had hit 6 degrees below zero. Yeah, Paula was actually pretty excited about an $800 night.

Since this Gordon fella didn't provide any contact information, Paula wasn't too worried about making sure she had the right drinks, appetizers, linens or whatever. He'd have to deal with what she has on hand. And she was the only one working, so his guests would just have to wait for drinks. So be it, she thought. Eight hundred bucks. Fuck yeah.

Paula turned some music on, flipped on the TV, plugged in the video game, and the jukebox, and went over to the bar to wipe down the counter to prepare the cocktail garnishes. As she finished her prep work, she looked at the clock on the wall and noticed it was 6:15 pm. The rental agreement stated that the bar would be available starting at 6:30 pm. Any time now.

Before she could finish the thought, the front door opened, and a bearded man barged in, bringing a gust of cold air with him.

Could this be my mysterious renter, she thought.

"Hey, are you Gordon?" she asked the man.

"No," the man replied.

"Oh, so are you *with* Gordon? Are you with his group? Because the bar is closed for-"

The man interrupted her. "I was invited. Can I get a damn beer?"

The man was being rude, and usually, Paula wouldn't put up with that shit, but since he's a guest of an $800 buck night, she didn't say anything to him. Paula went behind the bar and grabbed a beer glass.

"Greenline Brew, ok?" she asked.

"Fine," the man mumbled.

Paula poured the local brew into the glass and brought it over to where the man was sitting. "Do you have a name?"

"Not relevant," the man answered.

One of those customers, Paula thought. Usually best to leave that type alone and not engage. But Paula just couldn't resist. She never could. Challenge accepted.

"Nice to meet you, Not Relevant. I'm Paula," she said with a smile. The man only grunted in response and looked down into his beer.

At that moment, Paula decided to make it her goal to break through this guy's abrasive exterior to see what was underneath. It was a game that Paula and her staff would play every night – pick a difficult customer and try to turn them around by the time they left.

A smile was worth $5, and a laugh $10.

The bearded Mr. Not Relevant was going to be a fun challenge. Too bad her co-workers weren't there for her to collect, but it should be a fun night regardless.

Everyone's A Critic

The old clock on the wall chimed as the big hand reached the nine. "6:45. Looks like you're the only one so far," Paula said to Mr. Not Relevant.

Paula waited with anticipation to see if she was making progress with her new challenge. Nothing.

The front door flew open.

"You know, you could have better lighting out there. And that sign out front is crooked. And don't get me started on your website," announced the well-dressed, mid-30s man as he entered the bar.

"Hey, Mr. Overly Critical, are you in the right place? We're closed for a private event," Paula explained.

"Aw, really? Well, let me just grab a drink, then I'll be on my way," he replied.

"Yeah...I don't think so. Someone rented this bar at seven."

The man pointed to his phone. "It's only 6:46. Let me grab a beer, and I'll be on my way before the start of this massive event you have going on here," he replied while looking around at a nearly empty bar.

"Ha, ha. Ok, just one," Paula relented. "What'll you have?"

"How about a Guinness?" he said.

"Sure thing. What's your name? I'm Paula, and that's Mr. Not Relevant over there." Paula looked over at the bearded man to see his reaction. Still nothing.

"I'm Jeff. And sorry about the critiques as I came through the door. You know, small things bug me way too much. You have a nice place here. I've actually been here a few times," said Jeff.

"After a Cubs game?" asked Paula.

"Ha. Yeah, how'd you know?"

"Well, let's just say the designer pants and sweater over a $200 dollar button-down shirt kinda gave it away." Paula laughed, as she put down a fresh Guinness in front of Jeff.

"It's on the house. Enjoy."

Jeff laughed. "Thank you! Just for that, I'm going to write a great review of Rocco's Pub on Yelp." Jeff pulled his cell phone out of his pocket and opened up the Yelp app to type up his review.

"Rocco's Pub is one of the liveliest and best places in Chicago. Even on a Tuesday night in January, this place is hopping! Highly recommend. 5 stars! Submit." Jeff said aloud and then laughed.

"Thanks for that," Paula responded as she laughed along with him.

"How about you, pal? What's your name? Or is it 'Not Relevant, Man?'" Jeff asked the bearded man seated at the other end of the bar.

This got Paula's attention as she stopped taking the glasses out of the dishwasher and laughed at Jeff's version of her name for him. Still no reaction from Mr. Not Relevant.

"So, Jeff, what brings you here tonight? You on your way somewhere?" asked the curious bartender.

"Well, I was working late, and the damn EL broke down a block from here. Some electrical problem, so a bunch of us got off the train, and I came here for a drink. Hopefully, it's back working soon, but you never know with Chicago transit," Jeff explained. "But if you're giving away free beer, I just might stay all night."

"Don't get too comfortable. Again, someone rented out the bar for the night," Paula reminded him.

"Yeah, yeah, alright. Maybe I'll take one more before I go."

"Ok, one more. Let me know when you're ready." Paula conceded.

By now, Jeff had become fixated with his phone. Staring, typing, and scrolling. Paula had never seen such adeptness with a smartphone before. Maybe this guy could help her with her marketing, after all. Food for thought.

Mr. Not Relevant finished his beer, placed his glass down on the bar with an intentional thud, and grunted over at Paula. "Another?"

It wasn't really a question he was asking. More of a demand.

"I'm not so sure about that. You've had a few already. How about I get you an Uber instead?"

"Cut me some slack. I just lost my...job." Mr. Not Relevant replied with hesitation. Progress, Paula thought. He's speaking in sentences now. Best to engage while he's in the mood. Still miles away from a $5 smile, though.

"Oh shit, I'm sorry. What *did* you do for work? Maybe I know someone who can help? As the owner of this lively five-star establishment, I get to meet a lot of people." Paula replied as Jeff laughed.

Paula grabbed the glass from Mr. Not Relevant and put it under the tap to re-fill his glass after all.

"You can't give me a clean glass? *Really?*" The bearded man wasn't too keen on drinking out of a dirty glass, even if it was his.

Paula gave him a wry smile and continued to fill the used beer glass. Again, trying to goad him into talking and maybe, just maybe, crack a smile.

"So, what line of work are you in? Maybe I can help," Paula offered.

"There's no way you would be able to help. What I want. What I *need*, you can't exactly get on Monster or InNeed," Mr. Not Relevant explained.

"InDeed," Jeff interjected while still staring at his phone.

Paula was getting very excited now. Jeff had this guy talking, and it was only a matter of time before he'd crack a smile. Go, Jeff, go! Paula quietly thought.

"What?" the man asked.

"It's called In*Deed*. It's like the world's largest job site," Jeff said in a slightly condescending tone.

"Yeah, whatever. You won't find anything for me on there, either."

Paula, feeling the need to chime in and keep the conversation flowing, asked, "So, what's the mystery profession? Are you in organized crime or something?" Paula and Jeff both laugh again. Still nothing from Mr. Not Relevant. Not even an awkward, peer-pressure kind of laugh.

"You've been watching too much CSI," the unfriendly man replied.

"What!? No, man. For real. What do you *do*? Um...I mean, *did* you do?" Jeff asked again.

That question was apparently too much for the man without a name. He had reached his talking quota for the time being. He got up from the bar, grabbed his beer, and sat down at a round, low-top table about six feet away.

Jeff, looking up briefly from his phone, glanced over at the man, then back at Paula. "Hey, I tried."

I'm Gonna Be Rich

A woman in her early 30s was next to enter, and with her, a big gust of frigid cold air again filled the bar. This time, the door stuck in the open position due to the extremely high winds.

Jeff turned around to look toward the door and called out. "Whoa! How about closing that door?!" The woman quickly reached back for the door and pushed it shut - battling the brutal Chicago winds.

"Sorry about that, guys. It's cold as a witch's tit out there. And windy as fuck, too."

"Nice mouth," mumbled Mr. Not Relevant.

The woman, attractive, was dressed like she was on her way to a nightclub but somehow walked into one of the most ordinary bars in Chicago. With her fake fur coat, tight leather pants, high boots, and fishnet sweater, her kind was rarely seen at Rocco's. She didn't emulate the North Side vibe that usually frequents these parts. This woman was definitely a fish out of water.

The woman glanced at the man and walked over to the bar. Anticipating the woman would want something substantial to go with her bold personality, Paula asked, "What can I do for ya? Whiskey?"

"Hold on a second, babe," she replied. The woman reached into her knockoff Prada purse and pulled out an envelope. She opened the envelope and waved a printed invitation in front of Paula's face.

"Before we get to drinking, you can first tell me where I'm supposed to go for this. And then you can make me a Cosmo."

"Cosmo? Does this look like a Cosmo kind of place? You've come to the wrong bar for one of those, honey. The Viagra Triangle is about eight miles from here." This woman seemed much more at home in a place where creepy, old, wealthy, White men scouted for young gold-diggers, Paula thought.

"Your cabbie dropped you off in the wrong place, my dear. But, since you're here, how about a glass of chardonnay? We've got a vintage box of that stuff around here somewhere," Paula said with some snark. "But you can't stay long. Someone rented the whole place out tonight," Paula explained.

"Ok, fine. But what about this invitation?"

"What's that thing say?" Paula asked, motioning to the invitation in the woman's hand as she drained the boxed wine from the tiny plastic spout into a wine glass.

The woman took off her coat, threw it on the back of a barstool, and read it out loud in her strong Chicago accent. "Your presence is required at 7 pm on the third Thursday of January, two thousand and fourteen. Then it lists an address: 4131 North State Street. This is 4131 North State Street, right?"

"Yep, that's us. Rocco's Pub. Although I guess our sign out front could be, what did you say, Jeff? That it was crooked? I have bad lighting? I should just blow up the place and start over?" Paula teased Jeff.

"I apologized. I'm an ass, ok?" Jeff replied while laughing along with Paula.

Paula continued, "But I don't have any idea what that invitation thing is. Maybe someone is messing with you."

"I don't think so. Well, maybe. I don't really know. Look, someone went through all the trouble of printing this thing, ya know? This looks pretty fucking professional - not something you'd push out of a printer at home," the woman said.

Leaning in close to Paula, trying to convince her of her point of view, she continued. "Now, why would anyone go through all that trouble just to play a joke on little ol' me?"

"Sorry, sweetie. You aren't my type," admitted Paula.

"Your loss!" the woman replied.

Looking up from his phone, Jeff addressed the woman, who was now sitting at the bar two seats away from him.

"Maybe you pissed someone off, and they are getting back at you by sending you on a wild goose chase? Or maybe...just maybe. Naw."

"What!?!? Just maybe what!?! You can't stop there!" Now intrigued by the man's thinking, the woman wanted to know what Jeff was thinking.

"Well, I was going to say that maybe...whoever sent you this invitation isn't playing a joke on you, but they are going to give you a gift of some kind. I saw that in a movie once. You know, a mysterious package arrives at the front door. For the next two hours, they go on a treasure hunt, find a million dollars while encountering drug dealers."

"And of course, it's the drug cartel's money. Then they find out that the person's friend is kidnapped, and they have to use the drug cartel money they found to give to the kidnappers. Then the drug cartel catches up with everyone at the scene of the kidnapping and money exchange, and everyone - including you, little lady - is blown away in a final, bloody scene that Quentin Tarantino would be proud of."

"That's what that invitation thing is. Most likely. That's the night you have ahead of you. Probably." Jeff said while laughing.

"You may be cute, but you're crazy. There's no way this invitation ends up in a bloodbath. But I'd be ok with all of that money," the woman replied.

"Well, in all seriousness, maybe it actually *is* a gift of some sort. Not money or anything, but something else of value. Now that *is* something I saw on social media last week. People were giving gifts anonymously to strangers. Like a 'pay it forward' deal. Like when people in front of you in a Starbucks drive-through pay for your drink, then you do the same for the people behind you," Jeff offered.

The woman seemed very interested and excited about the prospect of getting a gift.

"Or, maybe you have a long-lost Uncle Matt, and he left you 10 million dollars. Or an Aunt Janet who had a rare coin collection, and she left it alllll to you," Jeff said, returning to the absurd to tease the woman.

She seemed to be buying into this line of thinking. "Yeah, that's probably it! I'm gonna be rich!"

Looking up from his beer and speaking in an angry tone, Mr. Not Relevant spoke again, killing the lighthearted mood. "Right. Sure. Your dead uncle Joe left you a billion dollars, and his estate lawyer printed up a fancy and mysterious invitation and wanted to break the exciting news to you here. At Rocco's Pub. On the coldest day of the year. Yeah, that sounds about right. I'm *sure* that's it. Fucking morons."

Hearing that, the woman got up from her seat, walked over, and sat right next to Jeff while looking at Mr. Not Relevant. "Well, I think this handsome fella is right. It's gonna be a big surprise for ME!" The woman put her arm through Jeff's and rested her head on his shoulder.

Jeff welcomed the affection, which caused him to momentarily take his eyes off his phone.

"What's your name, handsome?" she asked.

"Jeff. And yours?"

"Tiffany, but everyone calls me Binks."

"Of course they do," Paula said as she shook her head, smiled, and then brought the glass of wine over to where Binks was sitting.

"Thanks, darling," Binks said.

"Again, not my type," Paula replied.

"Hey Paula, I thought you said someone rented out this place at 7 pm tonight? Where's everyone? Maybe Binks's invitation has something to do with it?" Jeff wondered aloud.

"Yeah, I was thinking that it's connected, too. A few weeks ago, someone shoved a contract under the front door. They included a cash payment, paid in full for tonight at 7. Then the Binkster over there shows up with a printed invitation for the same night and the same time," Paula replied. "More than a coincidence, I'd say."

"It's 'Binks.' And who reserved the bar for tonight? Maybe that will solve this mystery. I am so confused. What is this is all about?" asked a perplexed Binks.

Paula tried to explain. "All I know is that a 'Gordon R.' reserved Rocco's for tonight. He paid a lot more than I would have asked, so I'm not too concerned if he's a no-show. Easy night for me."

"Well, I guess we'll find out the big mystery in five minutes," Jeff shared as he pointed to the old clock on the wall. "6:55 pm, and all the world's mysteries will be solved."

"I need another beer over here!" demanded Mr. Not Relevant in a grumbly voice.

Paula paused and thought about refusing the man another drink, but before she could think of something to say in reply, he spoke again. "Don't worry, I'm not driving. That would be beyond fucking stupid. I'll be getting a ride home tonight. That's for sure. That's *if* I go home at all."

"Good to hear it. So, if you don't go home, are you gonna go to a *laaaadies' house?*" Jeff and Binks both laughed along with Paula, but not Mr. Not Relevant. Instead, he appeared angered. This is going to be tough, Paula thought. The biggest challenge in a long time, for sure.

"I don't *have* a lady," the man said.

"Oh, that's cool. Hey, it's 2014. Sex is sex. Love is love. It's all good. Whatever floats your boat, as they say." Paula went back to putting clean glasses on the shelves behind the bar. More laughter from Jeff and Binks. Mr. Not Relevant just scowled and took a gulp of his Greenline.

Brothers McGee

The front door to Rocco's opened once again and in walked two men. One was holding a bright orange envelope, identical to the one Binks had. Both men walked over to the bar, and one of them held up the envelope.

"Hey there, I got this invita-"

Without letting the man finish his sentence, Paula snatched the invitation out of the man's hand and read it. "Your presence is required at 7 pm on the third Thursday of January, two thousand and fourteen at 4131 North State Street."

"Oh fuck, you're getting some of the money, too!?!" Binks said disappointingly.

"Money? What money? What's this invitation for? We both got one." The man pointed to the other man he walked in with. "This is my brother, Drew. And I'm Jake. Jake McGee."

"You *both* got one? Ugh!" Binks looked at Jeff and pulled her arm out from under his, knowing that he was likely wrong about this invitation and that she wasn't actually hitting the jackpot tonight.

Binks walked over to where Jake and Drew were standing near the bar and grabbed the invitation from Paula's hand.

"Fuck. I'm not gonna be rich! Especially since the McGoo brothers here both have one of these." Binks took the invitation and slapped it up against Jake's chest.

"Whatttttt the hell is going on? What do these invitations mean? Did everyone here get one?" asked Drew, as he spoke for the first time.

Paula answered Drew. "Just her, and you two. Unless Jeff, did you get one?"

"No, and I kinda feel left out," Jeff replied, staring at his phone.

"What about you, Mr. Not Relevant? You have one? And are you going to tell us your name now?" Paula tried again.

"Don't worry about it. And no. No invitation."

"Well, it's a few minutes before 7 pm, so I guess the three of you will find out what this means soon enough. In the meantime, what will you both have? The drinks are on Gordon R."

"I'll have a Bud Light and shot of Jack Daniels," Drew said. "Same for me," Jake chimed.

"You got it. Have a seat, boys, and I'll bring 'em around," Paula said, motioning to a low-top table.

Binks walked over to the men seated at the table and had a message for them. "So before you two fuckers showed up, I thought I was going to be rich. Jeff over there made me think I was inheriting a fortune from my Aunt Jane or something."

"What?? I was just having a little fun," explained Jeff from across the bar. "And it was Aunt *Janet*."

Jake, now talking to Binks. "Do you always talk like that?"

"Talk like what? You don't like my accent?" she asked defensively.

"Your accent? No, it's fine, I guess. But, the language. It's not, um, very lady-like," Jake clarified.

"Oh. Fuck that. I am who I am. By the way, I'm Tiffany, but everyone calls me Binks." Binks put her hand out to greet the two men. The three shook hands, and Binks sat down with the other invitation holders.

Paula brought over the beer and shots for the men and an extra shot for Binks and then gave Jeff one at the bar.

"Ok, really. How much do we owe you, Paula?" Drew asked.

"On the house tonight. It's a good night. Especially with what looks like a no-show from our mysterious Gordon R."

"Can I interest you in a shot, friend? On the house," Paula asked Mr. Not Relevant.

Without answering her question, he asked one of his own. "Are you always this generous with alcohol?"

"Not always, but we only live once, so why not, right? I mean, we are all adults, and this is now the age of Uber."

Mr. Not Relevant scowled at the bartender and replied, "No, I don't want a shot."

Paula refused to give up on her challenging customer. He was proving to be quite the adversary. "Ok, just let me know if you change your mind, fella."

"So, is your last name Rocco? Are you 'Paula Rocco'?" Binks asked, trying to be funny.

"Ha, no. It was my dad's nickname. Rocco. That's him and me in that photo up there on the wall. That was such a long time ago. I grew up in this bar, really. My dad loved this place. He used to talk about all of the fascinating people he met here. From athletes to celebrities and politicians to the regular people in the neighborhood. So many great people. Such great memories."

Paula started to get choked up before finishing her thought. "Anyway, he passed away 10 years ago and left me Rocco's. I've been here full-time ever since."

"Oh, that's sweet. Really sweet," replied Binks as a tear welled up in her eye.

Awkwardly and suddenly, Jeff spoke loudly to get the attention of everyone in the bar. "Ok, I have a small confession to make."

All eyes focused on Jeff, waiting for the big news.

"Are you Gordon R?!" asked Paula.

"No, no. I'm not. But I also have one." Jeff pulled a bright orange envelope out of his coat pocket, where it had been hiding.

"Damnit! There go the rare coins!" Binks said while dropping her head onto the table. Everyone laughed except Mr. Not Relevant.

"So, why hide it all this time?" Paula asked Jeff.

"Eh, I dunno. I first thought I was the only one with one of these things, then Binky shows up."

"Binks!" demanded Binks. "It's *Binks*."

"Yeah, anyway. I wanted to see how much fun I could have with *Binks*. But now I'm really curious. Especially now that Jake and Drew each showed up with one."

"What on earth could these mean? And why us?" Jeff asked as he held up his invitation to inspect it further, not expecting an answer.

Investigative Bar Theory

"Ok, there's got to be some reason all of you got that invitation. Let me see that again." Paula motioned to Jeff to hand him his invitation.

"Maybe there's a code hidden in the message somewhere," Paula reasoned and then read the content of the invitation slowly out loud.

"'Your presence is required.' Hmm, that's pretty straightforward." She went on. "'Your presence is required at 7 pm on the third Thursday of January, two thousand and fourteen.' This *is* January 16, the third Thursday, and it *is* 2014, so again, pretty straightforward. And there's nothing hidden in the address 4131 North State Street. I don't see any code hidden in here. Well, I'll be damned. It's an invitation *without* a secret code." Paula tossed the invitation back to Jeff.

Jeff had a theory. "I would have put my money on you being behind this, Paula. You know, create all these invitations just to drum up business. You get people intrigued with a clever ploy just to get them to your bar. I would have thought it was some super creative marketing idea, well, except for the fact that all of our drinks have been free. You'd be one dumb business owner if you came up with some clever ploy to get people here, only to then give everyone free drinks. My marketing brain was really confused about that approach to get new customers. If you are behind this, you really do need my help."

"You got me there, Jeff. I certainly didn't send those invitations. And I think I'll pass on the marketing offer," Paula replied with a bit of sarcasm in her voice.

"So, who sent them? Look, I don't have all night. I got people to see and do," Binks said before realizing how it sounded. Howling laughter erupted from the brothers and Paula.

"Um, I mean *things* to do and people to see. You fucking perverts!" Binks clarified.

The old clock on the wall chimed. It was the top of the hour. One...two...three...four...five...six...seven.

"Ohhhhh. It's the witching hour," Paula said with a girlish giggle of anticipation.

Everyone looked around the room, waiting for something, anything, to happen. After a minute or two of silence, Jeff got up from his barstool and walked over to the door, and peered out the window into the cold and dark Chicago night.

"Well, I don't see anyone coming. The streets are empty, and the wind is really whipping. Damn, it looks brutal out there."

"So, now what? Should we just leave? How long do college students have to wait for a professor to arrive to class? Is that still a thing?" Jake wondered aloud.

Drew, always one to add a smartass comment to anything his brother said. "Let's give it a few. Maybe something, whatever was supposed to happen at 7, is running late." Jake gave his brother a look.

"What? You don't know!" Drew responded in a loving and brotherly way by smacking Jake on the shoulder.

"Ok, kids. Enough fighting, or I'm going to send you to your rooms!" Paula said with a chuckle.

Paula seemed to be more curious than all of the others about the invitation and why these people were here. Maybe it was the fact that she was having way more fun than usual. Even the fun little side bets she and her staff would make weren't this exciting. Tonight would make a great story to share with her team tomorrow, that's for sure.

"Ok, let's try to figure this out. There's some connection between all of you. You guys don't know each other, do you? Maybe you know some of the same people, and that's how you're connected?" Paula asked.

"Yeah, the Six Degrees of Binky," cracked Jake.

"It's Binks, and I've got an idea. Let's play 20 Questions! It'll be super fucking fun! I love games!" Binks said excitedly.

Paula motioned to Mr. Not Relevant. "Hey, Mr. N.R., do you want to help us figure this out? It might take your mind off things."

The man replied in a grumbly voice. "No, I don't think that's possible."

"If you change your mind, sport, just let ol' Paula know, kay?" Still, nothing remotely close to a smile. Damn, Paula thought to herself. She'd met her match.

Paula turned her attention back to the others. "Ok, 20 Questions it is."

Paula walked over to the chalkboard menu she used to list the beer and food specials and erased everything written on it. "Here's what we'll do. We'll ask the same questions of all of you and write the answers on the chalkboard. There will *have* to be some connection between you. And we are going to have to figure this out ourselves, as it looks like our mystery guest isn't going to appear."

Paula created a simple chart on the chalkboard. "Ok, the first column Binks, second column Jeff, third column Jake, and fourth column Drew."

"The first question is to Binks. Ok, Binks, what do you do for work?" Paula asked.

"I'm an ER nurse over at County General Hospital."

"Oh God help us all," joked Jeff.

"Ok, ok. I don't think we need any commentary," Paula announced as she proceeded to write 'ER Nurse' under Binks' name on the chalkboard.

"Ok, Jeff. You're up. What do you do?" Paula asked, now playing detective.

"Marketing executive. I work for an agency downtown."

Binks, wanting to get in on the teasing, jumped in. "So, have you been on The Facebook all night? You creative types are always doing that social media thing. Big waste of time if you ask me. *Ohhh, look at me, I'm wearing a fancy new shirt. Oooh, look at these 27 pictures of my dog. Is it the cutest?* Vomit!"

"Yeah, something like that," Jeff replied, not wanting to take the bait and respond to any of her comments. Jeff was great at teasing others, but didn't take it very well when it was directed at him.

"Back to the chalkboard, people," Paula said. "We have 'Marketing agency' for Jeff. Drew, what about you? Job?"

"Well, I'm kinda not working a *real* job, but I'm an Uber driver." Looking down at his Bud Light and an empty shot glass, he clarified. "Well…I drive for Uber. But not tonight, of course."

Drew's reply briefly got the attention of Mr. Not Relevant. Paula noticed him look up from his beer and grunt but then immediately went back to staring into his glass. Something was off with this guy, Paula thought. She just didn't know what. Yet.

Turning her attention back to 20 Questions, Paula continued. "Ok, so Drew is an Uber driver," and wrote the same on the chalkboard.

"Ok, Jake, how about you?"

"I'm an attorney. I work at a large firm in the city."

Paula began writing on the chalkboard. "Ok, so Jake is a crook." Binks and Jeff both laughed, and Drew let out a howl. Listening to someone else make fun of his brother was the best kind of ribbing there was.

Defending himself and trying to enforce the rules of 20 Questions, Jake got defensive. "Hey, I thought we couldn't add commentary, Paula?"

"Right, right. Jake is an attorney, not a crook. Sorry, Jake. Ok, so we have a nurse, marketing exec, Uber driver, and attorney."

Paula and others contemplated the information on the chalkboard for a minute. And while they considered any connections, Mr. Not Relevant spoke in something other than a grunt. "Hey, barkeep. How about that shot now? And another beer."

Paula gave the man another once over and decided that he wasn't too far gone and agreed to give him a shot and another beer. She grabbed Mr. Not Relevant's glass, walked over behind the bar, and poured him another, and then filled a shot glass with Whiskey. Paula delivered the drinks to Mr. Not Relevant and then walked back over to the chalkboard.

"Alright. Anyone think of a connection yet?" Binks, Jeff, and Brothers McGee all shook their heads and mumbled no.

"Well, we're not related. So, there's that," Binks offered.

"Brilliant detective work there, Binks," Jeff replied.

"Ok, let's try this a different way. Has anyone been at County General in the last…Binks, how long have you been an ER nurse at County?"

"Three years. And before that, I lived in and worked at an ER in San Francisco."

"Ok, so let's say the last three years. Has anyone been in the County ER in the last three years? Either as a patient or visiting someone?" Paula asked the group.

Binks spoke first. "Well, I go there five days a week and every other weekend, but I get every third weekend off, and if I ask ahead of time, I can take a week off."

The others snickered, and Jake blurted out, "You've got to be kidding!"

"We know *you* do, Binks, but I was asking about everyone else," clarified Paula.

"Oh. Yeah. I guess that makes sense," Binks admitted.

"Ok. Anyone?" Paula asked again. Nobody spoke up, but instead, shook their heads.

"Ok, so nobody's been in the ER at County. I guess that's a good thing, but it doesn't help us with our mystery. Alright, how about our marketing exec Jeff. Anyone come in contact with marketing, um....*stuff* in recent memory?" Paula asked.

"That's not a real question, is it Paula? Marketing 'stuff'?? You can't be serious."

"Ok, fair enough. You might be a difficult one. Ok, everyone, get in Jeff's face and see if he looks familiar. Ok, go!"

Binks, Jake, Drew, and Paula rush over to where Jeff was sitting at the bar and got about a foot from his face. An uncomfortable distance for a stranger, never mind four at once.

"Get outttt!" Jeff said as he guided them away from his personal space. "You're fucking weird, Paula. And here I was thinking I'd help you market this bar and get actual paying customers in here."

Paula laughed and continued her detective work. "Ok, I got nothing. Anyone else?" Nobody knew Jeff. "Well, I guess you aren't very memorable, Jeffster." Paula wrote 'nothing' on the board in the Jeff column. Jeff shook his head, rolled his eyes, and diverted his attention back to his phone.

"Ok, Drew. Our intoxicated Uber driver."

"Seriously?!? I said I wasn't driving *tonight*!" Again, everyone except Mr. Not Relevant laughed.

"This is fun, guys." Paula was enjoying this night immensely.

"Ok, ok. So, has anyone taken an Uber in the last, let's say, a year or two. And if they have, do you recognize Drew?"

"Don't get up in my face! Personal space issues!" Drew offered preemptively, just in case they were going to pull another one of those maneuvers.

"Easy, boy," joked Paula.

"I never take Uber. Only Lyft. Because I loveeeee the pink logo!" explained Binks. "I'm partial to the pink."

Staring at his phone, Jeff offered, "Oh, I could go in so many directions with that one."

"Now, now. This is a family-friendly game," explained Paula.

"Well, obviously, I've been in Drew's car a lot. We're not just brothers, but we're also friends, so what does that say, Ms. Clouseau?" Jake inquired.

"Ha, good one. It doesn't give us much, however. Jeff, what about you? Do you think you've been in Drew's Uber?"

"I can't say for sure. I take Ubers all the time." Jeff turned around and talked directly to Paula. "Maybe there's a way for Drew to look up old passenger names? But even if he could, according to your super-sophisticated Investigative Bar Theory, wouldn't we all have to have the same thing in common? Like we would *all* have to have been in Drew's Uber? Binky over there says she only rides in pink cars, so that throws that one out the window, doesn't it?"

"Fair point, but I'm kinda making this up as I go, here. Bear with me. I'm a bartender playing detective, and this is the most fun I've had in a long time."

Paula went on with her investigation. "Ok, last but not least is our friend here, Jake, the lawyer. Has anyone been in trouble with the law? Been in jail? Rob a liquor--"

Jake interrupted her. "I'm not *that* kind of a lawyer. I'm a patent attorney. I ensure my company's products and services are protected by patents. You know. Inventions, intellectual property, and stuff like that."

"Oh, ok. So has anyone gotten into *patent* trouble in the last couple of years? Anyone?" Paula asked.

More laughs from the room, and this time, Drew high-fived Paula. "Oh man, I love you," Drew declared.

"Ok, so no patent troubles," Paula said as she wrote the same on the chalkboard.

Paula walked back about 10 feet from the chalkboard to get a different perspective and asked the group if they had any ideas at all. "Come on, guys. There has to be something connecting all of you."

Then suddenly, Mr. Not Relevant interrupted the silence and talked for the first time in a while. He got up from his seat and was now standing over a table in the middle of the bar. In a very deliberate and angered tone, he spoke. His voice shocked everyone. And frankly, scared them.

"What about *this date*?" he demanded.

Everyone in the bar turned their attention from the chalkboard toward Mr. Not Relevant, who seemed to be very relevant at the moment.

Paula was the first to speak. "What's that? What do you mean, *this date*?"

The man, who was mostly quiet until this point, was getting visibly angered and spoke again with a louder and more defiant tone. "This...fucking...date. January mother-fucking sixteenth, two thousand and nine!"

It was at this moment that Paula realized that Mr. Not Relevant had to be Gordon R. He's the one who reserved this bar. He's the one who printed the invitations and got all of these people here on this night. But why? Why did this man want all of them here on this night? She wondered. And she was frightened.

When Gordon R. Becomes Relevant

Gordon hoisted the table and with an upward thrust, sent it flying. The table flipped on its side and made a loud crashing sound as it hit the floor. The mood in the bar had drastically changed - from lighthearted to very serious – in a matter of seconds.

Gordon stumbled as he began to walk toward Paula. He caught himself by grabbing and holding onto the back of a chair. Three beers and a shot had an effect, but it was clear that he had been drinking before arriving at Rocco's. A man of that size would not be stumbling after only a few beers and a shot of whiskey.

What really shocked and scared the others was what they saw next. Gordon, still wearing his winter coat, pulled it aside and slowly raised his right hand. Secured firmly in his hand was a GLOCK 19 Gen4 pistol. The 9mm gun was illegal for civilians to own, as it was meant only for law enforcement. One of the more deadly handguns on the market, the weapon that could hold a full 15 rounds of ammunition, was now pointed in their direction.

"Shit! What do you want!!?" Paula asked. She was one of the calmer ones in the bar. She had seen her share of drunk, macho types over the years. Most of the time, these out-of-control men leave without incident. But this time was *very* different. The planning. The invitation. The $800 in cash. And the gun. This wasn't going to end well, she thought. Unless she could talk him out of whatever he's got planned. Remain calm, she thought. That was her best shot.

"Sorry, man. You are really freaking us out. What, what do you want? What do you want with us? And the gun. Surely you don't need that."

"Just shut the fuck up! All night I've heard you people talk fucking nonsense. Your stupid theories about how you're connected, your stupidly simple conversations."

"That guy is not a fucking lawyer - he *pretends* to be one to impress people. He flunked out of law school. And his brother there, yeah, he's an Uber driver, alright - but I'll get back to him."

"Binks over here *does* work at the hospital, but she's certainly not a nurse. She's a part-time receptionist and a full-time whore. Like, literally an expensive Craigslist call girl. What do you call yourself? What's the politically correct name for 'whore' these days, dear Binks?"

Binks was shocked and couldn't speak. Gordon stumbled and tried to maintain his balance. "And Jeff, the marketing executive? HA! Bullshit! He works at the casino, parking cars. As far as I can tell, he's never had a marketing job in his life. Maybe he just watched too much Mad Men as a kid. Is that what you tell the ladies, Jeff? Marketing Executive? Because a valet at the casino doesn't impress them enough to get them into the sack? Is that it, Jeff?"

Jeff was also too scared to speak. He'd never seen a gun up close before. Especially not one that was likely loaded and pointed at him. He was freaking out. They all were.

"And you, Paula. You are actually a bartender—the only truthful one of the lot. You are most definitely a bartender. You pour the drinks, and you dispense love advice, don't you?"

Paula wasn't sure what Gordon meant by 'love advice.' "I don't, uh, know," she replied.

"I thought I told you! All of you! To shut the fuck up!" Gordon stumbled a little closer to the table where Binks and the McGee brothers were seated and waved his gun in a back and forth motion.

"All of you. None of you-" Gordon began crying. "None of you have any right to say shit to me!" Gordon tried to compose himself.

"THINK! January sixteenth. Two thousand and nine!"

The silence was quickly replaced by crying and hyperventilating. They were all scared and confused by what was going on. The man with a gun was becoming unhinged, and nobody had any clue as to why.

Then it clicked. One by one, they all realized what was going on. And who this man was. A wave of realization and immense guilt consumed each and every one of them. Repressing bad memories and ignoring tremendous guilt is tough to do, and it takes hard work to keep that buried for five years. Once you train your mind to forget, though, horrible thoughts such as these can conveniently escape your mind and absolve you of the accompanying anxiety and guilt.

But at this moment, in Rocco's Pub, on one of the coldest nights on record in the city of Chicago, Paula, Binks, Jeff, Jake, and Drew all turned pale as they now feared for their lives. They had all unknowingly shared a deep, dark secret, but that was about to come to an end by a deranged man holding a gun.

They had spent the better part of five years pretending to be other people, but the facade was all about to come crashing down.

Survival Instincts

"Put all of your phones on the table. NOW! No bullshit tricks, or everyone's night will end real soon. And you, Paula, go sit with them." Gordon demanded while pointing at the table where Binks and the McGee brothers were sitting.

Gordon collected all the phones and put them in his coat pocket. He then walked over to Jeff, who was still seated at the bar. He waved the loaded gun at him again. Rage had overcome Gordon R.

"You, Marketing Guy. Fancy wanna-be marketing guy with your designer clothes and fancy haircut. Where were *you* on January 16th, five years ago? Surely you remember!"

Jeff, barely able to speak with a loaded pistol aimed squarely at his head. "I-I was working. At the casino. Probably valeting cars. What do you want with me?!? What did I do to you?!?"

"What do I *want*? What did *you* do to *me*, you ask? Tell me, Jeff, how many cars do you park every night?" Gordon demanded.

"What? Um. I don't know. Maybe 30 cars for each of us if there's two guys," Jeff responded.

"So, 30 cars every night. And how many nights do you usually work in a week, *Jeffff*?"

"I really don't know. It varies, I guess," Jeff replied, not knowing if he was providing the answers that Gordon wanted to hear.

Gordon was now louder and pushed the gun closer to Jeff's face. "Give us a guess, Jeff!"

"Stop it! What did he do to you, you fucking monster!" Binks interjected to defend Jeff. She quickly realized that was probably not the best idea.

Gordon swung the gun around and pointed it at Binks. "I'll get to you later. For now, keep your mouth shut!" Gordon turned his attention back to Jeff while still pointing the gun at Binks. "Come on, Jeff, how many nights?"

"Four! Four nights a week," Jeff said with urgency and an attempt to divert the attention and gun away from Binks.

"Four. So 30 cars a night and four nights a week. That's 120 cars every week. You park them, then run and get them and give them back to their owners, right?"

"Yeah, I suppose so."

"What do people do after you take their car from them?"

"What do they do?? What-? I mean, um. They're in the casino. Gambling. Maybe seeing a show." Jeff answered, again not knowing what Gordon was looking for and afraid that if he gave what Gordon perceived as the wrong answer, he'd...well...Jeff didn't want to think about what Gordon would do.

"That's right, Jeff. You are doing so well now. Now, what else happens in that casino?" Gordon asked, slightly slurring his words.

"What do you mean? Gambling, mostly. But I park cars, so I'm not too sure."

"You can't think of anything else? Come on, you're a creative *'marketing guy'*. Surely you can think of other things that might happen inside a casino."

Binks interjected again, but this time she was trying to help Jeff instead of telling Gordon to back off. "I know there are private rooms where the ladies-"

"Yeah, you'd know all about that, wouldn't you? But no. Not that, Binks." Gordon turned back to Jeff. "What else, Jeff? People have a good time, don't they? What condition are people in when they return to get their cars from you?"

"Well, yeah. Lots of people have a good time. A lot of them have been drinking," Jeff admitted.

"And, there it is! Jeff, I *knew* you could do it. Great job. People actually drink in the casino. Now, Jeff, out of those - what did you say - 120 - people who you see *every* week?" Gordon asked, still waving his gun back and forth as he spoke.

"Yeah, about that."

"So how many of those 120 people would you say come out of the casino, *sober*?"

"Oh, I really don't--"

"Jeff, we aren't going to go through this again, are we? Give me a fucking number."

"Sober. Well, completely sober. Probably about 10 people."

"Ten!" Gordon declared. "Ten people who come and get their cars from you are sober?"

"Yes."

"Do sober people tip well, Jeff? Surely the expert marketing team of valet parking attendants you hang out with all talk about who tips the best, right? You know, like Paula here has her little games she plays with bar patrons. Little side bets and such," Gordon said while he looked over his shoulder and made eye contact with Paula.

"So, Jeff, I ask again. Do sober people tip well?"

"Once in a while, but no, not really."

"Well, as my Uncle Willy used to say, 'Now, we're cooking with gas.' You're doing so well, Jeff. Ok, so we've determined that only about 10 people out of 120 you see every week are sober. And those 10 people are most likely *not* good tippers. Am I doing ok, Jeff? This sounds right so far?"

"Yes, but I still-" Jeff caught himself before finishing his thought.

Gordon stumbled around the room between two of the tables. He slowly walked past where Binks, the McGee brothers, and Paula were sitting and then turned his attention back to Jeff.

"Ok, so what about the other 110 people? Is it fair to say that there's probably a decent number of those people who are just a little buzzed but not too bad? Is that fair?"

"Yes, that sounds right," Jeff replied.

"And, would you agree that this group of slightly buzzed people are better tippers than the sober ones, Jeff?"

"Probably, yes."

"*Probably*, yes? Jeff, I think you can be a little more definitive than that."

"Yes. Definitely better tippers," Jeff confessed.

"Ok, so what does that leave us with? Anyone?" Gordon asked as he looked at the others. Nobody knew if Gordon wanted an actual reply or if it was another rhetorical question. The wrong answer could be catastrophic.

Binks answered anyway. "Really drunk people who are great tippers."

"Wow. Now that little lady gets a gold star. No, no in fact, I think she gets a free drink. She was looking for gifts a little while ago. Rare coins or whatever. Let's get our friend Binks here a drink."

Gordon walked over to the bar where the bottle of Jägermeister was still sitting. He grabbed a beer glass and filled it halfway. He walked over to Binks and slid the glass to her. "Drink it."

"There's no way. I can't drink all of this. I'll get sick. I just-." Binks said as she started crying.

"Drink it. Or die." Gordon demanded.

Drew stood up quickly from the nearby table. "Hey man, you can't-."

Gordon swung around and pointed the gun directly at Drew. "Sit the fuck down, Uber boy. This doesn't concern you." Gordon turned back to Binks and repeated it. "Drink it!"

Binks, crying and shaking, struggled to manage just a sip. There was no way she could finish all of the nasty-tasting Jägermeister.

"All of it." Gordon added.

Paula put her arm around Binks and whispered something in her ear that seemed to calm her down a little. Binks composed herself, cleared her throat, and then steadily drank the syrupy black licorice drink until it was gone.

"Now, didn't that taste great?" Gordon sarcastically asked her. Binks ignored the man and rested her head on the table, and sobbed. Paula again consoled her while Gordon walked toward Jeff at the bar.

"Ok, so we've determined that there's a group of very good drunk tippers who constantly emerge from Jeff's casino."

"It's not *my* casino-" Jeff said reactively. Gordon gave Jeff a look. Jeff told himself at that moment that he shouldn't speak any more than absolutely required. What a stupid thing to have said, he thought.

"So, Jeff, tell us, what's the best tip you've ever received?"

"$100. Some rich guy from the Emirates."

"Good for you, pal. How about the people who aren't rich and from the Emirates? What's a really good tip from someone who is pretty fucking wasted? Tell us. Maybe we can all get jobs parking cars."

Jeff thought for a second and answered honestly. "I'd say about $50 or so."

"$50 bucks!?!? Wow. Just to get their car? That's quite a tip for driving someone's car a few hundred feet. Why do they tip you so much? It's truth-telling time, Mr. Marketeer."

This presented another instance when Jeff had no idea what Gordon was looking for. He couldn't afford to get it wrong, so he said the first thing that came to mind. "Well, a lot of them insist on driving home. Nobody wants to leave their cars at the casino. They try to convince us they're ok to drive."

"Aha! There we have it! They *try* to convince you that they're ok to drive. But are they? You know they can't drive safely, right, Jeffy boy? They're trying to convince you, but they're slurring their words, aren't they - kinda like I am right now? And they really shouldn't be driving, should they? You and your car-driving pals know this, right?" Gordon demanded to know.

"Yes, we do," admitted Jeff.

"So these drunk people, who shouldn't be driving under any circumstances, are tipping you pretty big sums of cash, and you look the other way? Isn't that right?"

"Well, they all signed a waive---" Jeff replied, still not able to hold back.

"Jeff!" Gordon screamed as he pounded his fist on the bar. Binks cried louder, and Paula let out a shriek. Drew and Jake started to get up from their seats to spring to Jeff's defense but quickly sat back down after realizing that Gordon hadn't moved on Jeff or fired his weapon. Yet.

"Yes! Yes! OK!?" Jeff pleaded with Gordon.

"So, for the slow ones in the back, let's summarize what our friend Jeff here was doing five years ago on this very day. He was marketing. Wait, no, my bad. He was *parking* cars at the casino and accepting big tips from drunk casino customers. And Jeff was just letting them drive off because, well, because the tips were good. That, ladies and gentleman, is our friend Jeff."

Gordon walked over to the chalkboard, grabbed a piece of chalk and crossed out what Paula had written. "I think we need to make some changes on this board, don't you folks? I think it should read 'Jeff takes money from drunk people and lets them drive' in the Jeff column. Anyone disagree?"

Nobody spoke.

"Yeah, that's what I thought."

Gordon walked over to Paula. "Paula, Paula, Paula. Tell everyone what you were doing five years ago on this very night."

"Well, I must have been here. Working. I only have a handful of employees, so I work most nights," Paula was confident in saying.

"Ok, so let's just say you were here that night. Here at Rocco's serving your free boxed wine and Jägermeister shots to anyone who wandered in. But do you remember anything about that night specifically? Did something happen in your *personal* life that night?"

Paula's face turned white as she gasped for air. She tried to speak, but the words wouldn't come out. All she could utter were three words. "Oh my god!"

"Yeah. I thought so. I'll come back to you later," Gordon promised. Now Binks, feeling sick from the liquor, tried to console Paula as something had clearly changed.

"You two!" Gordon said as he motioned to Drew and Jake McGee. "You two make me want to put all 15 fucking bullets from this GLOCK into your sick little heads. I was tempted - so many times - to just end your miserable lives before tonight. But for some unknown reason, I resisted. And here we all are."

"I truly don't know what you mean," Jake replied.

"Oh, I think you do. I think you both do. Haven't you figured it out by now? I know you fellas aren't all that bright, but come on. You didn't just forget, did you? Was it *that* insignificant? Do you usually pick up drunk women from the scene of an accident and dump them in an alley *near* a hospital on a regular basis?"

"Oh fuck!" Drew said while turning to Jake. "I told you we should have called 9-1-1! Fuck!"

"Ohhhh, yes. 'Oh fuck' indeed, my little friends. Ladies and gents, not only do we have the famous McGee Brothers, but we have Drew here, who shows up at the scene of an accident, where it was obvious that the driver of the vehicle was drunk out of her mind. A woman who was lucky to walk away alive after hitting a telephone pole. A woman who totaled her car and called a cab to pick her up. And the brilliant Drew here not only picked her up but agreed to take her to a bar. Not a hospital, but a *bar*. Isn't that right, Drew?" Drew was shaken and couldn't speak.

After a slight pause, Gordon answered his own question. "Yes, you sure did. And what a coincidence that the bar she wanted you to take her to was none other than the beautiful establishment we find ourselves in right now, Rocco's." Gordon explained as Paula sobbed.

While the fear in the room was palpable, the others didn't know why Paula was reacting so strongly to this part of Gordon's story. But their questions were about to be answered.

Things were getting really scary. If there ever was going to be a time for the others to act and save themselves, it would have to be soon.

"But why here, you ask? Why did *my wife* want to come here? Well, that's an excellent question, Gordon. But I'll share that little nugget last of all. Because it's a doozy," Gordon said aloud, talking to himself.

The pieces of the puzzle were beginning to come together. Why this drunk, angry man had invited all of them to this bar on this night.

Gordon continued. "So Drew picks up a drunk woman, sees her totaled car, doesn't call the police, but called his *brother* to get advice on what to do with a wasted and injured woman in his cab. A woman who had just climbed out of a totaled car. So, what did Drew and Jake decide? Take her to Rocco's Pub and let her be someone else's problem. But it was, what, about 10 minutes later that you noticed she wasn't breathing? Is that right Drew?"

Not leaving any pause for Drew to reply, Gordon kept going. "So, at this point, you now notice you have a *dying woman* in the back of your car, so what do you do? You called your boss at the cab company, right? 'Hey boss I have a woman who's in pretty bad shape in my cab'. No, no, you called 9-1-1, right? Drew called 9-1-1 in an attempt to save my wife, right? That's *surely* what he did, because he certainly wasn't going to let her die!" Gordon again answered his own question.

"Well, to end the suspense for everyone, no, he didn't. Drew didn't call his cab boss or 9-1-1. He didn't do any of those responsible things. He called his brother again! Because, you know, that's pretty much the same thing, isn't it? Now, exactly what happened next is a little fuzzy to me. There's only so much information that cell phone tracking data can provide."

"But ultimately, these two fucking Einsteins thought the best course of action was to take a passed-out, blind drunk woman to a bar. A woman who had just nearly killed herself by smashing her car into a telephone pole. These assholes thought it best to dump her in a dark alley *near* a hospital and *hope*. I guess '*hope*' that someone would find her?"

"Is that what the plan was, genius brothers?"

The brothers couldn't speak. They knew their lives were likely over. Immense guilt and regret consumed them, just like it had whenever the memory of that night surfaced. But they had gotten better about avoiding it by repressing the memories and pretending it never happened.

They had all done their best to forget that night. But that was over now. Tonight, they were facing their demons, and his name was Gordon.

"Was it that you didn't want to be responsible or helpful or, oh, I don't know...SAVE A PERSON'S LIFE by taking them *all* the way to the emergency room?"

"These model citizens, these pillars of society, decided a better course of action was to leave her in an alley. Maybe neither of you cared if she lived or died. Maybe you didn't give a shit if she choked on her own vomit, or if she died due to massive internal bleeding. Or was it that you just didn't want to get involved. Wash your hands of this inconvenience that was my wife? Does that about sum it up, guys?" Gordon asked, and this time he wanted an answer. "Well?"

"We thought for sure she'd be found. We looked for a spot where people would walk by." Drew offered as their reasoning. That's the best they had for an excuse.

"Stop! Just fucking stop! I've thought about this very moment every day for the last five years. What I would say to you. And what your reasons would be. Your excuses. Nothing would come close to being acceptable, but maybe, just maybe, one of you could offer some type of logical reason for dumping a helpless and hurt drunk woman in a dark alley. But I should have known better than to expect more from you."

Gordon now stood next to Jake and had the barrel of the gun pressed up against his forehead. "Two lowlife brothers didn't have a good reason whatsoever. They just didn't want to get involved."

"Nooo, don't! Please don't!" Drew screamed while the others yelled similar pleas. Gordon backed away from Jake, walked over to the chalkboard, and wrote, 'dumped woman and left her to die in an alley' under and across both brothers' names.

Gordon turned away from the chalkboard and focused his attention on Binks. "This is where you come in, isn't it, sweetie? Good ol' Binks makes her appearance now, doesn't she?"

"I swear. I tried to help! I gave her CPR, but she was already gone. And I-" Binks stopped abruptly.

"You what? Tell us," Gordon asked in a somewhat calm voice.

"Well, I had been out that night. I got off work at 9 pm and met some friends out. We went to a party, and well, I ended up accidentally doing some coke," Binks said, and for the first time, without the ditzy accent she had all night. She was hoping nobody had noticed the slip.

"Oh, that's rich. Accidentally doing coke. I'd love to see how that *accidentally* gets up your nose. In fact, you are a regular user, aren't you? You were on your last strike at County General, isn't that right, Binky? Isn't that how you lost your previous hospital job in San Francisco and why you changed your name from Michelle to Tiffany? And within your first year at County General, Tiffany here was caught twice in random drug tests, and she was told one more strike, and she was OUT! Gone. Fired again. Isn't that right, Binks, Tiffany, or Michelle, or whatever it is that you are calling yourself?"

Binks, now crying, tried to explain her reasoning for her actions that night. "Personnel records are surprisingly easy to obtain when you have a badge," Gordon explained.

"I-I tried to help her, but she was already dead!"

Gordon wasn't having it. "You were coked out of your fucking mind. Did you really know she was gone? Don't you think there was at least a small possibility that she *wasn't* dead? That you, in your scrambled frame of mind, maybe you weren't thinking straight? That maybe, just maybe, she could have been saved by someone else? Someone who had actual medical training and who wasn't high as a fucking kite?" Gordon's somewhat calm demeanor was short-lived.

Binks cried uncontrollably. The kind of crying where you try to catch your breath but find it difficult to breathe.

"But, no. You left her there for fear of getting caught using again. Getting that third strike and losing your job *again*, you decided to let her sit there in an alley where the fucking brilliant brothers had dumped her. Again, *to let her die.* Does that sum up your role in this pretty accurately?"

Binks was still not able to speak. Crying and gasping for air. "I'll take that as a yes," Gordon replied for her.

Something was noticeably different. During Binks' grilling, Paula had gotten up and moved to a different table to sit by herself. She was no longer interested in comforting Binks. The others noticed this and wondered why. With a drunk madman waving a gun in their face, they couldn't afford to contemplate it for long, but they had noticed a drastic change with Paula.

Gordon walked over to the chalkboard, crossed out what Paula had written about Binks, and wrote, 'cokehead whore leaves dying woman to choke on her own vomit.'

Paula was now crying. While everyone at Rocco's was understandably traumatized by the evening's events, nobody was quite sure how Paula fit into this horrid tale. But they were about to find out.

"And that leaves Paula. You know, for the longest time, I was under the impression that you were her yoga instructor because that's what she told me. That's the little plan you two came up with, wasn't it? You aren't a yoga instructor, as well all know. You're the owner of this fine establishment. Maria mentioned you quite a bit. 'Oh, my new yoga instructor Paula is the best. She pushes us hard in class and knows how to get the most out of everyone.' 'Paula is having a special midnight yoga session tonight to celebrate 10 years in business, and she only invited her best customers.' She went on and on about you. You and Maria met at Mind&Body Yoga, and that's where it all started, didn't it?"

Paula felt the need to provide Gordon with the truth. He deserved it. Everyone had been lying to him for five years. At least she could be truthful now, she thought.

"She told me she was unhappy and that you two weren't getting along—and you were headed for divorce. That's the only reason I pursued anything with her."

Appearing calmer again, Gordon leaned over and spoke kindly to Paula. "You know, I don't blame you at all. Maria was an incredible woman. She'd do anything for anyone, no questions asked. Maria wore her heart on her sleeve and gave all of herself to others. She was an easy person to love. So I don't actually blame you for anything. I blame all of them."

Gordon and his gun turned back toward the table with Binks and the McGee brothers.

"Maria would never allow anyone else to drive drunk, no matter what kind of money anyone would throw at her. She would never have left another human being in a cold, dark alley because they didn't want to get involved and to *hope* someone else would find them."

"Maria would never leave someone sitting in their own vomit for fear of getting in trouble or fired. She was the most giving and loving person I had ever met. She was so much better than all of you put together. And now she's gone, and each of you played a part in her murder."

Gordon turned back to Paula. "I don't blame you for loving her. Or her for loving you. I just wish she had told me. That's one thing about Maria. She was a pleaser. Always wanted to help others but never did much for herself. She was so full of kindness. So many people loved her. The people at her funeral. There must have been 300 people there that day."

"I know. I was there." Paula said through her sobbing.

"Yes, I saw you in the security footage. It caught you signing the guest registry. You made her happy where I couldn't. You filled a void she had."

Paula wanted to come clean about everything. "But that night. On January 16, 2009. We got into a fight."

"Whatever argument you two got into, I'm sure, was really about Maria and me. We had a disagreement that morning. She tried talking to me, but I was fucking stubborn. I believe that she was trying to tell me about you, but I refused to listen. And she left upset. She said she'd be gone a while, and when it got late, and I hadn't heard from her, I got worried. She wasn't answering her phone, and none of her friends knew where she was. I never thought about looking for her at the casino. The casino is where we met more than 20 years ago. Looking for her there never occurred to me."

While Gordon was reminiscing about Maria and discussing Paula's relationship, Jeff, Binks, and the McGee Brothers noticed that Gordon's gun wasn't in his hand any longer. During the discussion with Paula, Gordon had placed the gun on one of the empty tables, halfway between where Binks and the brothers were sitting and where Jeff was seated at the bar.

The time was now. This was going to be their best chance to make a move. If this didn't work, they'd be dying tonight. Even with a plan, they could die anyway, but doing something was better than doing nothing.

And in that moment, none of them saw the irony.

Jeff and the brothers formulated their plan. With non-verbal cues and eye contact, the men were ready, but they had to wait for precisely the right moment. A time when Gordon was distracted or if he looked in a direction away from the gun. They needed just one small opportunity to act.

Gordon went on. "I checked the yoga studio, her favorite coffee shop, Target, and even the library, where she often spent time clearing her mind to think. But she wasn't at any of those places. I never thought of the damn casino. I've replayed that night in my head so many times. If I had only checked the casino."

"But I've also been thinking a lot about you people for the last five years. If only *one of you* had an ounce of decency. All it would have taken was one fucking ounce. Call 9-1-1, drop her off at the ER, or I don't know, don't let her drive drunk to begin with. But you fuckers didn't possess such decency. You still don't. And you don't deserve mine."

"Was she perfect? No. But she was kind and loving and a wonderful person. She had a bad day, and I take responsibility for that, but you people. You are responsible for her death. Maria didn't deserve to die, and the four of you don't deserve to live," Gordon declared.

Gordon noticed that his gun wasn't in his hand but on a table several feet away. He hadn't remembered putting it there, but there it sat. He must have put it down when he was talking to Paula, he thought.

In what seemed to happen in a fraction of a second, Jeff motioned to the brothers and mouthed 'now!' as they made their move. Jeff jumped off his barstool and ran to the light switch on the wall behind the bar. One of the brothers went for the gun while the other lunged at Gordon.

In an instant, the bar was dark, followed by a series of loud crashes. There was a struggle. Tables and chairs were thrown about and slammed on the wooden floor.

The sounds of men yelling and furniture crashing was quickly followed by two loud gunshots and a woman's high-pitched scream.

The More Things Change

The sun was shining through the windows of Jeff's Bar, illuminating its dusty and unkempt interior. Jeff unlocked the door and entered.

He took off his coat and hung it on the rack by the door. He walked over to one of the tables, removed two chairs from their upside-down position, and put them on the floor. He took a rag and cleaned off a thick layer of dust from the tabletop and chairs. He then went behind the bar and found the remote to turn on the TV, half wondering if the old relic would turn on or if the batteries in the remote still worked. "Success!" he muttered to himself.

The front door of the bar swung open. 2019 had only just begun, but Chicago seemed to be breaking low-temperature records daily.

"Damn, it's cold! Not sure it's been this bad in years," Michelle said as she walked over to the bar.

"Oh, hey, babe. Yeah, it's a brutal one, that's for sure. What'll you have? How about a Cosmo?" Jeff asked with a cynical laugh. That joke never gets old, he thought.

Michelle took off her coat and sat down at the bar. "Funny guy. You know I'm working in the ER tonight. I brought a Diet Coke, anyway. Gotta wash down the nasty stuff with something. And I wouldn't want anything you have sitting behind that bar, anyway. So when do the others get here?"

"Any minute. Didn't you notice that I put 7 pm on the email invitation?"

"Ha, of course I did. Nice touch." Michelle looked at the clock on the wall while digging through her purse for her phone. "Well, that thing isn't helpful. What time is it?"

Right on cue, Jake and Drew walked through the front door, and with them, more cold Chicago winter air.

"Maybe I should fix that door," Jeff said to Michelle as the brothers walked in. "Then again, maybe not for as little as we use this place."

"Usual seating arrangements, I see," declared Jake, as the brothers exchanged greetings with Michelle and Jeff, then took a seat at the table that Jeff had cleared for them. Both men kept their coats on.

"Well, it looks like we're all here. Can we make this one kinda short? When it's this cold, Uber gets real busy. I could make a killing tonight." Drew said to the group.

"Six below wind chill! Why do we live here again?" asked Jeff.

"Kids!" Jake replied. "And yeah, I gotta run, too. It's movie night for the wife and me," Jake added.

"I think we can all say that we hate this weather," Jeff interjected. "But, these shots should warm us up," he added as he poured the liquor into the shot glasses.

"Can't we switch it up this year? I mean, *Jägermeister*? Does anyone even like this stuff?" Drew complained as the others shared their disagreement with his idea. As if they were going to change things now.

"Ok, ok, I know. It's tradition," admitted Drew.

"And it would be bad luck to change our annual toast now. I mean, it's been five lucky years for us, so we can't screw up our mojo because of one little shot of nasty licorice every year," said Michelle, who was on her way to work at County General.

"That's right, honey!" Jeff replied as he leaned over the bar to kiss her.

"Ok, raise your glasses, boys," Michelle said.

Jeff walked around the bar and joined the others as they stood and raised their glasses for their traditional toast.

"May this day serve as our annual reminder that loose lips sink ships and that we are only as strong as the bond we share through common secrets. Until next year - The 116 Club!" Michelle toasted.

"The 116 Club!" the others replied.

They downed their shots and said a quick goodbye to each other. The brothers quickly filed out of the bar with shouts of "*See ya next year.*"

Michelle lingered a bit.

"I'll see you at home after my shift." Michelle leaned over the bar to give Jeff another kiss. "You staying long this time?"

"Oh no. Probably not. I'll close up in a few," Jeff replied.

"Great. See you later, *Marketeer*!"

"Smartass! Be safe, hon."

Michelle put her coat on and headed out the door, but the door didn't stay closed. Jeff walked to the front of the bar and slammed it shut.

Alone in the bar again, Jeff walked over to the table where the McGee brothers had been sitting, wiped it clean, and put the chairs back on top.

He walked back over to the bar, grabbed the TV remote, and turned up the volume. The TV was playing a wildlife documentary about rare, wild cats.

The narrator of the documentary sounded a lot like Richard Attenborough, Jeff thought. He liked the way British voices sounded, especially with documentaries. They sounded more believable or something. He turned up the volume loud enough so he could hear it.

"It's a particularly skilled species of feline that only needs to annually escape from its hidden lair to forage and kill in order to survive. And once this endangered species has achieved its goal, and it has enough food to sustain life for the year ahead, it goes back into hiding - keeping well hidden from inquisitive and dangerous predators."

Jeff turned off the TV and put the remote back where he found it, walked over to the front door, turned around, and looked back into the bar. "The 116 Club. Until next year," he said aloud.

He then switched off the lights and exited the bar for the last time.